Daisy's Crazy Thanksgiving

S0-AUY-676

Margery Cuyler
Pictures by Robin Kramer

Henry Holt and Company   New York

Text copyright © 1990 by Margery Cuyler
Illustrations copyright © 1990 by Robin Kramer
All rights reserved, including the right to reproduce
this book or portions thereof in any form.

Published by Henry Holt and Company, Inc.,
115 West 18th Street, New York, New York 10011.
Published in Canada by Fitzhenry & Whiteside Limited,
91 Granton Drive, Richmond Hill, Ontario L4B 2N5.

Library of Congress Cataloging-in-Publication Data
Cuyler, Margery.
Daisy's crazy Thanksgiving / by Margery Cuyler ;
pictures by Robin Kramer.
Summary: Wanting to spend a quiet Thanksgiving away from her
parents' restaurant, Daisy discovers that her relatives lead even
crazier lives than her own.
[1. Thanksgiving Day—Fiction. 2. Family life—Fiction.]
I. Kramer, Robin, ill. II. Title.
PZ7.C997   1990
[E]—dc20   90-4323

ISBN 0-8050-0559-5 (hardcover)
1   3   5   7   9   10   8   6   4   2
ISBN 0-8050-2348-8 (paperback)
1   3   5   7   9   10   8   6   4   2

First published in hardcover in 1990 by Henry Holt and Company, Inc.
First Owlet paperback edition, 1992

Printed in the United States of America

For Daisy Rockwell, in mutual celebration
of many fine family parties   —M.C.

For my Dan   —R.K.

D aisy lived with her mother and father over Rockwell's Café.
Every night, she helped them in the family restaurant. She
made leafy green salads. She set the tables. And she helped with
the dishes.

Most of the time, Daisy liked working. But on holidays, she was miserable. She had to make twice as many salads. She had to set twice as many tables, and there were dirty dishes piled from the floor to the ceiling.

One year, Daisy said to Mama, "Thanksgiving is almost here. I'd like to visit Grammy and Grampy. I never get to see them on holidays."

"I'm not sure you'd want to," said Mama. "Thanksgiving at their house is a zoo. The relatives come, and they're all crazy. When they get together, they're even crazier. I know, I grew up with them."

"Well, the restaurant gets crazy, too," said Daisy. "Especially on Thanksgiving."

Mama bit her lip. "I suppose you could try it . . ."

"Please!" said Daisy.

"Even if it is a zoo, you probably do need a change . . ."

"I do!" said Daisy.

"I'll call Grammy and Grampy tonight," said Mama.

On Thanksgiving Day, Aunt Millie picked up Daisy in her new truck. Two Great Danes, three cats, and a pet monkey were hanging out the window.

"Time to go, dearie," squealed Aunt Millie.

Daisy climbed into the front seat and started to sneeze.

"I'm allergic to cats," she said.

"Here, have a hanky," said Aunt Millie.

All the way to Grammy and Grampy's, the dogs barked, the cats hissed, and the monkey pulled Daisy's hair.

When they drove into the driveway, Grammy and Grampy were outside painting the house.

"Come inside and meet the family," said Grampy.

Daisy fell over her cousin Tommy, who was playing with his pet lizards on the floor.

"Do you want one?" he asked, leaping up.

"Come meet your cousin Filamena," said Grammy.

"Hi," said Daisy.

Filamena burped, then grabbed some cereal and smeared it on Daisy. She ducked and ran into the living room, where Uncle Joe was doing his exercises.

"One, two, three, four," he panted.

Daisy leaned down so that her face was inches from his.

"Hi, Uncle Joe," she said.

"Hi, Grammy," he answered.

"I'm not Grammy," said Daisy. "I'm your niece, Daisy."

"Whoops," said Uncle Joe. "I don't have my glasses on."

Daisy's cousins, the twins, were leaping up and down on the couch, shouting at one another.

"Hi," said Daisy. But they couldn't hear her. They were making too much noise.

"Dinner!" called Grammy.

Everyone squeezed into Grammy and Grampy's small dining room.

"Where's the turkey?" asked Grampy.

"I'll get it," said Uncle Joe, heading for the kitchen. A few seconds later, he came back.

"I looked in the oven," he said, "but the turkey looked raw."

Grammy clapped her hand to her head. "Oh, no!" she moaned. "I forgot to turn the oven on!"

"Good!" shouted Grampy. "I hate turkey. Let's have pizza. Millie, call Jerry's Pizzeria and tell them to deliver ten big ones. With all the extras. And lots of garlic."

Aunt Millie jumped up and raced out of the room.

Daisy's stomach rumbled. She was getting very hungry.

"Let's dig into the vegetables," said Grammy.

She and Grampy heaped the plates with broccoli, sweet pota-toes, and stewed tomatoes.

"Stewed tomatoes make me sick!" said Tommy.

Filamena burped.

One of the twins reached for the bread basket, and knocked over Daisy's glass of water.

"You spilled water on my new dress!" shrieked Daisy.

"So what?" said Tommy.

Daisy shoved the soggy vegetables around on her plate.

"Pizza for everyone!" shouted Grampy as Uncle Joe and Aunt Millie brought it in. "Pass your plates!"

Daisy bit into a slice and gagged. Anchovies—ugh!

The doorbell rang. "Sorry I'm late," said Aunt Josie. "I had to give Billy Boy a bath."

"I like your outfit this year," said Aunt Millie.

Billy Boy jumped from Aunt Josie's arms and scampered under the table. The Great Danes raced after him. The table trembled and shook and lurched. Billy Boy streaked to the kitchen and the Great Danes followed. Food, dishes, and silverware flew everywhere.

Aunt Millie's monkey jumped up on Uncle Joe's shoulder. "Get that furry ape away from me!" he yelled. Tommy rescued his lizards, just as they were about to be gobbled up by Filamena. All three dogs came charging back into the dining room, barking so loudly that the windows rattled.

Daisy put her hands to her ears and ran upstairs to Grammy and Grampy's bedroom. She quickly dialed the number of Rockwell's Café. Papa answered.

"Get me out of here!" wailed Daisy.

"Mama's already left to pick you up," said Papa. "She called to wish you a happy Thanksgiving, but when nobody answered, she got worried."

"It's so noisy here, you can't hear the phone," said Daisy. She hung up and dove under the pillows.

A half hour later, Mama arrived.
"Want some pizza?" asked Grampy.
"Want to do push-ups?" asked Uncle Joe.
"Want to hold the monkey?" asked Aunt Josie.
"Want to play with my lizards?" asked Tommy.
"Want to paint?" asked Grammy.
"Want to jump on the couch?" asked the twins.
"Want to hold Filamena?" asked Aunt Millie.

"I just want Daisy," said Mama.

" 'Bye," said Grammy and Grampy. "Come back for Christmas."
Daisy kissed them and got into the car.
"I missed you," said Mama.
"I missed you, too," said Daisy.

When she walked into the café, Daisy found piles and piles of dishes in the kitchen.

"I wash, you dry," said Papa, handing her a towel.

They worked quietly until all the dishes were done.

Finally it was time for their own Thanksgiving dinner.

Mama and Papa brought cold turkey and other leftovers to the kitchen table.

"I'm sure glad to be home," said Daisy, reaching for a drumstick. "Grammy and Grampy's Thanksgiving is really crazy."